mid-size housewife

tara m. givens

table of contents

the concentric

clear breeze collides on
clean skin, whispered calm
behind days hazy in my
unclean respire, our

sediment, the sun shows
brief and satisfied; clavicle
conduits resettling in
rhythm for our very heart.

a movie star,
off clock;

hair aflame,
from habit.

leaving dc general

two nights in that trench:
my urgent stay at the did-drop
inn; the only building bound
to have held me, the wife
of a taxpayer.

in my room with brenda,
the grinning toothless:
rubbing mayonnaise
on her face as if
it were vaseline;

in our vestibule, she
rocked in government issue
carpet pad- for she, too,
was not a taxpayer.

in my room with brenda,
to whom i gave my cloak, my
cloroxed duvet-
without which, i'm told,
i refused to leave my home.

my last night in tie and
yield, wheeled out when
'not our problem': the
warm ambulance sped me
politely, uptown.

a new mouse in old traps,
learning the labyrinth yet;

we shall both wear these
new capes.

the schizophrene

he came lurching, seamless
in darkening distance: each pull
of our cigarettes bore him closer-
a mescalined crab, scuttling
sideways smooth over the
grassy field, his human scale
over the high chain fence, he was
before us: himself, roaring
for requite from our mother,
who had already drank
to sleep.

my eyes failing in focus, the slip
of metal from his pocket- my sister
hooting her "motherfuckers",
laughing with the *here-we-goes*
as she flicked her butt, standing now
in double-socked k-swiss shoes
because he'd called her the n-word,
grandly suggesting she
fellate him.

my palsied brain, then;
half in the slow motion
of loose orchestrated
movement-my sister

dueling at disadvantage
in his one-sided sword fight
as i straddle his back- fists
pounding the minotaur
as he spun, trying to stab
his own head.

the other half-a-mind
a shutterbox, capturing the
fleeing, our feral feats
of survival; visceral
unfettering of the
rage that we were
shoved so violently
into always fighting these
battles-never-ours.

the dread vacuum
of our victory
swan-sung
from a side-stage seat;
on beige carpeted stairs,
our mother wails
apologies,

only heartbreaking
to the untrained ear.

the black knight

black lincoln (continental)
black leather seats
my somewhat
    unfamiliar
grandfather
with a sister
and a cousin:
three furtives in
natural scowls.

we lost our balance
with ice cream cones;
an inevitable failure,
    the *no-turning-back-nows*
passing between the back seat
as we all seemed to brace
    for a man's beating.

his foot lifts for the brake
    reaching above decidedly-
the strangest fist.

sliding the sunroof, he said to stand

and wiping the ice cream, he hummed a tune-
without taking his eyes off the road.

after racquetball

a hot black beater,
ripped vinyl seats-
hot punctuations
        against

sweaty and sunburned
legs in cut-offs,
arms in   guns n' roses
with the sleeves
rolled up.

reaching in and
        unlocking
        the door.

the interior
marinated,
fresh asphalt
steam-heat stench
        and muffler exhaust.

the blood trapped
at my jawline,
veins constricted
indoor blast A/C
after
        improper cool-down.

the pee came out

driving into georgetown,
my bladder clenched on
borrowed time, when
tragedy struck twice.

a fender bender in the box-
an insurmountable gridlock;
the hospital a quarter mile away,
and three lifetimes.

oh, indifferent machine:
slow-turn stoplight,
your greens, and yellows.

the reds.

oh, this cannot happen.

still, from somewhere unfelt,
the quiet draining of the dam-
a cascade of steady humiliation,
a giving up.

the horror of knowing that even in
ordinary emergencies,
my body would commit such
crimes against me.

false-legged uncle

my father's brother stayed
in his mother's attic;
behind the
white people projects,
built on
the other side of town.

a house proudly-graveled,
with its band of
mostly-smiling
outlaws;
tragically loyal,
familial tie measured
not by what they did,
but to whom
it was done.

i would bring the
sauerkraut and sausage
up the stairs,
averting from all the
HOT BITCHES!
on brown-paneled wall,
the scotched tape
poorly applied,
and reapplied-

false-breasted
torsos,
neatly folded into
poses for the

lowest common denominator:

citrus neons on
sun-warped skins,
the begging dominance
purchased, so falls
more flat-

leaving me
casually disappointed,
unexpected *deja vu*
but still filing it;
a seven-year-old's
unnoticed osmosis.

downstairs,
inviting clouds feeding
from filter-less
pall-malls
and the
strange dust
from black shag:
an overlit darkness
with bare bulb
in daytime.

we cruised his
1980 camaro with
dusty yellow stripes;
electric wires on
wooden poles
coated in pollen,
waiting for

cool breezes.

mylar flags mapping
perimeters of a
cracked parking lot;
the unspoken man
who sold us
worm tequila
at the register.

then idling and
stopped by
train signal:
red lights
flashing pattern
in bored urgency,

red optic beatbox
paired with the
once-hot-pink promise
of GIRLS
against plywood
black-painted,
flashing ahead
between train cars.

i knocked against
the hard plastic of his leg-
"only charity ever took"-
grayed as an old man's
thumbnail,
and equally ridged;

texture-dulled smears
of the same graphite
that settles even
upon the people,
this side of town.

with the
open window scent
of gasoline and
hot gusts of
the *out-of-doors*,
which is not
nature:

"let's jump the train,"
i say, and quietly
wondered how he
lost his leg.

a sly side-grin,
his voice chuckling
over the lewd and
obsequious exhortations
of david lee roth:

"let's not and say we did,"
and in misunderstanding
i also grinned,
eyes staring through
t-top,

prepared for takeoff.

lovesick

i found myself running
toward a cliff, so
desperate for a loss
of gravity that i
jumped, just to feel
a gain.

the firmness of my breath in
negative, the velocity into
which comes the *before*
before of *overcame.*

the pull of *mother*; a
bitter fruit fallen
from handprint trees, the
cracked neon plastic
bleached in the sun.

the weight of *wife*; a
constantly replayed trick, the
emerging from the
bowels of *family*
not covered
in shit.

grafting myself to some
fleeing pod-seed, a
slip of the *then she*
like a shedded snake

over oklahoma

in her cloak like nature, she holds
her pattern: imploding in cyclone
to churn her earth; in blasts of
concrete, she might scream
the houses, the whip of wet
wheat; the drape of her hard-
won sediments.

her mottled orange sometimes
in no sun, but pinks that seem
to hold it, still.

you could lose a person, in that
short horizon.

pusher

it was the wind.

it was me.

an aluminum reflection in
your stunned eyes, i am
frozen forever in
wide-eyed and
blinded reach,
backdropped
in unforgiving
sunlight.

at impact,
a deafened
and complete
implosion,
repeating on smaller scale
as your body reverberated
on parched rock.

slow-motion disbelief
perceived you-
the final rebel,
dying in
disgraceful arcs
without the dignity,
the smooth-lead kiss,
of the bullet.

black box mangled,

splayed flat
and heavy

but for a feather
once jaunty,
you are
enveloped now:
well-scented breezes

carry your spores,
imperceptibly mounting
in a diaspora
of strange and
unprepared cilia.

a reverie of coffee-laced tongues

i would have liked to crawl into you,
i would have liked to be your
glowing skin with my star-
crossed eyes, gazing.

you were the rain that
washed my crime
away, you came
grinning, you
were the crack
of lightning,
come to part
the storm.

you lift
through my
house, you are
a majesty in
utero, you
are kneeling.

you are the moss- you
have swallowed me, just as
the tree swallows the squirrel;

i can smell you and smell you.

blink

under a hazy glow,
low-watt bulb
with tightened throat;
shallow breath
arouses lust,
and want.

hiding under
lazy tongues.

parched for shimmer
with enchanted casanovas
lapping at my toes.

maneater

the diagonal of
our body
a double helix
of a double x;
sultry and curved
as the arachnid,

two tagmata desperate:
rabidly rejoining to one.

nightspeak

my red streak melting:
playing under easy dress,
fingers smearing beauty
over skin.

the flood aches frantic,
inside barely crushing heave
(red wants beneath, always);
she bleeds through.

the moon keeps swimming:
gripping angry angel grace-
he takes my head for mad,
drifts away.

catsuit

in pulse behind
fast whisper, she is
in the snare; her
obstruct forms
a riffle:
the numeration in my
discards; a scoring of
my bones.

at the surface the only sound
a firm-gripped zipper tug-
an invisible encouraging hand,
pulling against the final teeth;
comfort that settles at the
last, my

purple-eyed cheshire:
dealt into the chaos, and
reshuffling the bridge;

guiding the turn
until each card stands-

a single file, rising

as i pass.

mother's lament

'come on, little piggies, come, come, rush, rush!'
mother calls from the kitchen, to the three of us;
in her green apron with scarves in her hair,
she has fancied the table and ushers us there.
then dad runs down, yells "shut the front do-ah!!",
and brother blames the dog for the mess on the floor.

solutions

a soft splash of soap
from inside: deep
neon lavendress,
in silky calm.

her comforted dazzle
rainbowing heaven in
kitchen light at noon- she is

not ferocious, swirling
in the bleach: she steams
on the walls, her smile
polishes the sinks

bifurcative

please, living with my double-heart
beheading crickets chirping fine
leaves of grass.

of all the animals, the finest she has
in lavender hills, Royal purple blood
in

these veins.

extractor

his waterfall winched, beats out
the welded bits of my own
questionable metal- *this*,
this is stainless steel, *this*
is surgical.

the crack of his seal, a knuckle
cranked open into the ribs, he only
handles in screw for coin- no
kiss; he knows

only my fabric, my
ninety-pound capacity.

fumes

the indelible night stamp swapped
for liquid fear amping up gas-cycled
cyclones in the furor's looking glass.

green air rain for the road, asphalt
glistens in day oil, spread and slickened
like sicily on a day trip.

they might never sleep but
they sure will
get there.

no one asked to
see my papers.

distress

the shutterbox grinds;
       mind encapsulated, slight

           affords of honey.

varsity

squirming around behind me,
behind heavy glass doors,
behind- way behind-
the quasi-suburban houses
covered with mud:
gasoline chokes the kids
in their howdy-doody
yee-haws; plastic
picture junkies
smile bright under
perfect parts.
gleaming teeth
mask ectoplasmic
late-night
vomits
quiet in
soft orange
nightlight,
cold knees numb,
clenched fingers
gripping pink bunny
from the double canopy
of the barbie doll bed.

delirium

to the synapse clipped in unseen rotation,
to the lightning raid on loosened trapeze,
come sly fetter, the dear manifestation-
my faceless ancients: my sisters siamese.

our airborne arcs, an ageless grace
as we traverse the changing gradients;
in black smears, our flourescent trace-
the fauvist's pulse of radiance.

sirens gathered in reckless shimmer,
a bacchanal of exploded heart-
until at once no light glimmers;
the beauty of multiplicity departs.

then shroud in nostrum, obscuring the glow-

i belong to all turns of the pole.

pillar-tops

slapping at my feet screaming, *do not fall-*
mind shorn clean: still stolen balance throughout;
each time thinking, *i should have shown them all.*

urged back to pose with st. rubin, et al.,
legs a-palsy in accompanying drought;
slapping at my feet screaming, *do not fall.*

when i have roiled backward, then cleaned the wall-
shimmed sideways on my spine to gaze about;
each time thinking, *i should have shown them all.*

tether-rags dyed, early dress for the ball-
i dance slow, stung: numbed rebound from clout;
slapping at my feet screaming, *do not fall.*

and swear not *here* will i choke on my gall-
a world in chaos, i'll wring to wear out;
each time thinking, *i should have shown them all.*

ratcheting bones in over-angled haul-
no print for the season's uncompassed rout:
slapping at my feet screaming, *do not fall*;
each time thinking, *i should have shown them all.*

dirty diamond

oh, sister grim: haute mistress,
wont fool; hex of my octahedron-

i'll show you.

heretics

for days i unshackled, passing
pneuma through my body, washing
hundreds through my veins, bruised
knees in their repentance, bending these
unhallowed bones; old souls unleashed,
the demons made indignant- mockmen gnashed,
lashing my grip in the defiance, whipping the
sound into the walls.

for nights i scratched at doors marked
holy, my cries echoed for the priest, a man
trained to ease the rack of this war; still falling
in atonement, scoured in lye, through water
that never rinsed clean, for weeks walking backward,
in
Fact that i was His, my injured feet running
for a cross, or any sign of a way; my twin
twice gasped in thunderbolt, casting
light upon the horror:

the wood there stained in his own
violent submission, the stones that had
stacked his open grave, women who dared
at night to free him, and returned in daylight,
to make sure he had run.

it goes this way always; the confessions
in fast whisper, the silent girding of the
gift, the ignorant violence at the hands
of small men: only an unhewn spirit can endure.

spirals

i found the phone cord,
nurse, you
child; boy bold at
first crack in power:
you split my bone, nurse,
with your idiot needle.

they patched me through,
nurse, you
sack peasant, you
rough strapper, you
denied to me my
hands, refused me the
courtesy of your
hateful name.

hello, richard.

my left eye framed
in your plexiglass
as you turned, my
raw mouth wide-
inhaling your
'jesus'; i
crushed my
hissing throat in
twists, in
testament to the
unreasonable survival
of my body and of
what it can do, my

only weapon, this
laughing-stock.

the pulling of it
away as if its
smile could
kill you.

your heart

you taste like cyanide
lapping through skin
and burning my eyes.

you love disease.

i broke marilyn's record,
fading in hollywood;
i was still dying on our
silver screen,
when you tore it down.

the moon still hums your name.

blanch

arms overhead she is pushing,
staring beneath, watching it rise
as he slides the spectrum,
boiling red to swirling black.

porcelain breaks into arch
to wrap around hard lips;
sliced thick and sliding fast
against his mounting,
sharp arms stung white.

his grin ripping insides-
she falls through a fire;
another cripple of death,
in slow motion.

karoshi

the heart of america,
i tore what i could–
and ate it on live t.v.

the healed amnesiac

off the ground where i'd collapsed,
my heart and bones were ailing-
in shadow dance and strange eclipse,
half-buried from her flailing.

echo of fistfall on quick-locking door
(am i machine or marionette);
peering through a fractured lens
upon bleached and black vignette.

mute rainbow of tulle, fitfully torn
reveal corsets carefully stitched-
sewn up since she was born;
she had not seemed bewitched.

on her skin the bubbles burst,
as she slides under the steam-
hidden under milky twirls
of jasmine and shaving cream.

a sick sweet-tooth capped with gold,
no root left to unbind;
in her eyes, no story told-
and i have been left behind.

mermaid eating air

my mind has a clever tilt,
it has done as it has pleased.
and just as an altar built,
so can it be seized.

the smiling sea and his pure bent
holds me in his sway;
not knowing how his tide foments-
he likes to watch me play.

a sudden shift in dolphin spin,
an anchor dropped in dark;
wires slapping water din
electric in my heart.

surfacing in crooked dance,
i grabbed for every wish;
throwing back a wicked glance,
and slaying all the fish.

then up to reach the burning stars
i thought were mine to take,
scarcely feeling unsealed scars
left gasping in my wake.

nadir

the tin-foil shiver of touch
on fevered skin; the
strangeness of the slack,
pulled tight.

a clinical excavation,
isolating pressure points,
a gloved palpation from above
finding my sharp edges,
my crystal root-

a pocked marble then,
lifted to squeezing height
(an unnoticed zenith)
and in such position
that just the one drop
had shattered it.

dropsy

through the wetted hoods of sanity,
a constant flood of facts; in
deluge of vulgarity,
the obliterate chokes
         and gasps.

out of the ground

my baby peppermouth spits
thorns through these holes
in my teeth.

such fire i once did breathe-
every lick tore through this skin,
now slack and wasted:

crouched as moving shadow,
a blind fury dressed as an
armor of rage.

i was not scared.

then up from darkness, a
thrust of white coat: my
shrunken form dipped in
false patina, the naive range
of prognoses; an attempted
amniosis.

reformed now, a portrait
breathing with bended limb;
my profile in glass as i walk

through vacuums that
smell of winter, with only
these thorns inside.

my baby peppermouth sleeps.

of all the people

you are but a mouth in the mass,
a sow with your sheeple,
sloshing piss in the grass.

showing teeth when you swallow
some sad story of late;
in your own shit you wallow-
a pig never stays sate.

your grunts break the peace
as you twitch your big ears,
your stupid eyes increasing:
a bruised apple's appeared!

your judgements are gnawing
where food will not ease;
enough with your mawing-
you spread social disease.

i won't roll in your back-talk,
down swill with your bevy;
why, you can't even walk-
your bowels are too heavy!

on the rag

because that's the only time
people recognize emotion, but
only as temporary insanity; an
inside joke made plain, a
fine excuse for those who say,
"i am strong because i feel nothing,"
and hold mock for those who bleed.

catlady

in the shrinked curio of
my tiny attic, my tiny totems
all finally aloof, and well-
proportioned; i hide
the little things in my
clothes as if they were
survivors,
feeding them bits
of dry steel wool to
keep their bellies.

the ladies of valhalla

i.
a relic of the ages- when all was screamed
and fast; i was hostage, bound to translate sounds
in my house, burning down, not one thought more
than the function of my body; i bought a
lifeline, called you 'the couch'.

then heaving in blindness, blocking the path
for years, our insides distended; the jolts
of us punched back to place: me, always
in zippers or seams- not figuring in
failure; but how could you have, just as
the children had gotten so loud.

hiding the matters in your horrible folds, dull
cerumen of gritted feet on pink canvas, sheening
under jellied toast crumbs; draped in rags of
emotion, discounts so stretched, in time that
the mice could run through.

i was caught out scissoring the wires, refusing
to think straight- barely blunted the slivered
edge, the hard curl of my own skin; i
needed you that far then, away from me, i
shrugged: deep.

ii.
i was too small to lift you, still snapping
bones on the joints, yet like springs
loaded, trampling us to the curb- my stitched
body wept where you'd skid

metal into me; i rested the half of us
on the hydrant, paused to wipe my
blood: pitiful, how we had looked, in our
outsides.

the strangers came in sunlight to steal your
parts, matching islands to your stains, glanced
back often, afraid at the animals
i might keep; recalling their names for it,
what i had let savage you, left feasting
on foam inside your hanged under-
belly, unsupervised.

and moved away smug, having verified
you- garbage, knowing your type- having
inspected you already for value or bored
with clues, no question: you were
ruined out here- clothes spun,
off at odd angles, you squatting there
naked, in shoes, waiting for the
city to come.

so you could call out with each
upheaval- the lonely odors you'd
expect, the periodic toppling in some
landfill, ingesting discards of every era- there,
in freeze-frame, bent at the knees, always

eating the lime; as when it was law
to burn us, or wait until we floated: sometimes
this is best, still i dream myself valkyrie, chosen-
chopping even small pieces smaller, clenched;
sifting you into lighter bags- the fibers of me

awake in feint.

iii.
in the windows flagging, i yelled out the
help i needed, dropping strange accents
and waving; demanded to recall the
hearse, stealing us backward inside
as if you were mail: all the neighbors,
watching.

cutting you out of nylon before they had yet
bent you down, shooing off the
people, the smells of the lifting; flicking
bleach- you were mine, again: i had
tools already in your ears,
stabbing.

piercing swift, the rip of your
layers in scores, at shoulders and
hips; the pronounce sharp all the way to the
wood, determined you would have
good bones and could carry your
weight, could hold yourself even,
when dissolved.

tweezing plastic and dropping coins, working;
blowing brains at how you had stood, holding
all my tiny skeletons, sand crushed beneath
spread and uneven padding; fumes tore my
eyes for when i'd cursed their resolve, or
thought that they were food.

you, unalive- or breathing the darkness; not

undulating terror, here we can eat off floors,
supported; always clean or close, and never
impatient, but 'the sofa', though
we're only pieces here: we don't
call names.

mid-size housewife

why would we travel to rake circles in a quiet man's sand, when all we need to sift can be found under the household rugs, if you use your bare and wet hands, and the blisters come from the work, not the tools.

it does not matter how much flesh is lost, nor if the work was very hard or very easy:

you were alive.

Made in the USA
Middletown, DE
22 September 2022

10750391R00035